I Can Read!™ BEGINNING 1

THE FIRE CAT

Story and Pictures by

ESTHER AVERILL

HarperCollinsPublishers

HarperCollins®, 🐾®, and I Can Read Book® are trademarks of HarperCollins Publishers.

The Fire Cat Copyright © 1960 by Esther Averill Copyright renewed 1988 by Esther Averill All rights reserved. No part of this book may be used or reproduced in any manner whatsoever without written permission except in the case of brief quotations embodied in critical articles and reviews. Printed in the United States of America. For information address HarperCollins Children's Books, a division of HarperCollins Publishers, 1350 Avenue of the Americas, New York, NY 10019.
www.harpercollinschildrens.com

Library of Congress catalog card number: 60-10234
ISBN-10: 0-06-020196-7 (lib. bdg.) — ISBN-13: 978-0-06-020196-8 (lib. bdg.)
ISBN-10: 0-06-444038-9 (pbk.) — ISBN-13: 978-0-06-444038-7 (pbk.)

❖

Contents

PICKLES

Once upon a time,

there was a yellow cat

with black spots in his fur.

His name was Pickles.

Pickles was a young cat.

His paws were big.

And he wished to do big things
with them.

But where could Pickles find
anything big to do?

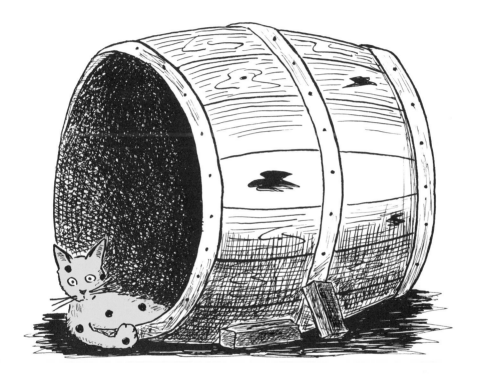

Pickles lived in a barrel.

The barrel was all that he had

for a home.

Pickles's barrel was
in an old yard
where there was
nothing big to do.
So what did Pickles do?

He ran after little cats.

He ran after every little cat
that came into the yard.
And he chased the little cat
out of the yard.
This was a bad, bad thing.
But it was all that Pickles
could find to do.

Next to Pickles's yard was a house.

In the house lived many cats

who called out to Pickles,

"You are bad.

You cannot be our friend."

But Pickles did have a friend

in the house.

His friend was Mrs. Goodkind.

Every day Mrs. Goodkind came
into the yard and gave Pickles
something to eat.

One day Mrs. Goodkind said,

"Pickles, you are not a bad cat.

You are not a good cat.

You are good and bad.

And bad and good.

You are a mixed-up cat.

What you need is a good home.

Then you will be good."

Mrs. Goodkind picked up
the mixed-up cat.
She took him into her home
to live.

In Mrs. Goodkind's home there was a pretty chair for Pickles to sit on. There were toys for him to play with.

But Pickles did not want

to sit on a pretty chair.

He did not want

to play with toys.

So he ran back to his barrel

in the yard.

And he began to chase

the little cats again.

Mrs. Goodkind said to Pickles,

"Things cannot go on like this.

Something will happen."

The next day
Pickles chased
a little cat
up an old tree.
He climbed
after her.

Pickles sat up in the tree

near the little cat.

He would not let her climb down.

After a time, the wind began
to blow.

It blew and blew and blew.

And the rain came down hard.

It came down harder and harder.

At last Pickles let the little cat
climb down and go home.

Pickles wanted to climb down, too.

He wanted to get back
into his barrel.

But he could not climb down.

Sometimes this happens to a cat.

And it happened to Pickles.

Mrs. Goodkind ran
to the tree.
"Pickles!" she called.
"Please try
to climb down."
But Pickles could not
climb down.

Mrs. Goodkind ran into her house.

Pickles could see her

by the window.

She was talking on the telephone.

Then she called out to Pickles,

"The firemen are coming!"

A fire truck came up the street
and stopped at Pickles's yard.
Three firemen jumped down
from the truck.

Mrs. Goodkind came
out of her house.
She ran to the firemen,
and pointed to Pickles.

The firemen put a ladder
against the tree.
One of the firemen began
to climb up the ladder.

The fireman climbed

to the top of the ladder.

"Come, cat," he said to Pickles.

"Let me help you."

The fireman picked up Pickles

and tucked him into his coat.

Then he took Pickles

down the ladder—

down to Mrs. Goodkind.

"Mrs. Goodkind," said the fireman,

"is this your cat?"

"No, Joe," said Mrs. Goodkind.

"Pickles has no home,

and he does not want

to live with me."

"Why?" asked Joe.

Mrs. Goodkind answered,

"My home is too little for Pickles.

Pickles is a cat who wishes

to do big things.

And someday he will do them.

Look at his big paws."

Pickles put out a paw for Joe
to see.

"My goodness, Pickles," said Joe,
"what big paws you have!"
Pickles looked at Joe and said
the one word he could say:
"MEOW!"
And Joe could see
that Pickles wanted
something very much.

Joe gave Pickles a pat.

"Pickles," he said.

"I will take you to our firehouse.

Maybe our Chief will let you stay."

THE FIRE CAT

Joe took Pickles to the Chief,

who was sitting at his desk.

"Oh!" said the Chief.
"I know this young cat.
He is the one who chases
little cats."

"How do you know?" asked Joe.
The Chief answered, "A Fire Chief
knows many things."

Just then

the telephone

began to ring.

"Hello," said the Chief.

"Oh, hello, Mrs. Goodkind.

Yes, Pickles is here.

He came with Joe.

What did you say?

You think Pickles would like

to live in our firehouse?

Well, we shall see.

Thank you, Mrs. Goodkind.

Good-bye."

The Chief looked at Pickles
and said, "Mrs. Goodkind says
you are not a bad cat.
And Joe likes you.
I will let you live here
IF you will learn to be
a good firehouse cat."

Pickles walked quietly
up the stairs after Joe.

Joe and Pickles went into a room

where the firemen lived.

The men were pleased to have a cat.

They wanted to play with Pickles.

But suddenly the fire bell rang.

All the firemen ran to a big pole

and down they went.

The pole was the fast way to get

to their trucks.

Pickles could hear the trucks

start up and rush off to the fire.

Pickles said to himself,

"I must learn to do

what the firemen do.

I must learn to slide

down the pole."

He jumped and put his paws

around the pole.

Down he fell

with a BUMP.

"Bumps or no bumps,

I must try again," said Pickles.

Up the stairs he ran.

Down the pole he came—

and bumped.

He tried again—and bumped.

But by the time the firemen

came back from the fire,

Pickles could slide

down the pole.

"What a wonderful cat you are!"

said the firemen.

The Chief did not say anything.

Pickles said to himself,
"I must keep on learning
everything I can."
So he learned to jump up
on one of the big trucks.

And he learned to sit up straight

on the seat while the truck

raced to a fire.

"What a wonderful cat you are!"

said the firemen.

The Chief did not say anything.

Pickles said to himself,
"Now I must learn to help
the firemen with their work."

At the next fire, he jumped down
from the truck.
He ran to the big hose,
put his paws around it,
and tried to help a fireman
shoot the water at the flames.
"What a wonderful cat you are!"
said the firemen.
The Chief did not say anything.

The next day the Chief called

all the firemen to his desk.

Then he called for Pickles.

Pickles did not know

what was going to happen.

He said to himself,

"Maybe the Chief does not like

the way I work.

Maybe he wants to send me back

to my old yard."

But Pickles went to the Chief.

At the Chief's desk stood

all the firemen—and Mrs. Goodkind!

The Chief said to Pickles,

"I have asked Mrs. Goodkind to come

because she was your first friend.

Pickles, jump up on my desk.

I have something to say to you."

Pickles jumped up on the desk

and looked at the Chief.

Out of the desk the Chief took—

a little fire hat!

"Pickles," said the Chief,

"I have watched you at your work.

You have worked hard.

The time has come for you to know

that you are now our Fire Cat."

And with these words, the Chief

put the little hat on Pickles's head.

THE OLD TREE

Pickles made friends
with all the firemen.
But he did not make friends
with any cats.
When cats came to the firehouse
to look at the trucks,
Pickles chased them away.

The Chief called Pickles to him
and said,
"A Fire Cat must be kind
to everyone.
You must be good
to other cats."

Little by little, Pickles learned
to be good to the cats he met.
He made friends with them, too.

Then all the cats loved

to come to the firehouse.

On rainy days, most cats stayed
at home, and Pickles sat upstairs
with the firemen.

One rainy day, as he sat there,
he thought to himself,
"How bad I was when I chased
the other cats.

Once I chased a little cat
up a tree.
Oh, me! Oh, my! Why did I do that?"

Suddenly Pickles heard the Chief
call out, "Cat in a tree!"

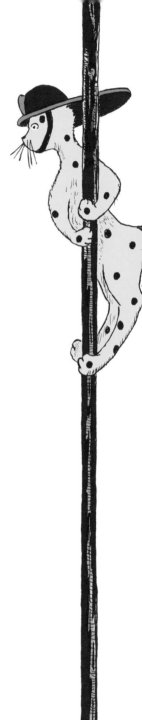

Fireman Joe
and two other men
slid down the pole.
Pickles slid down
after them.

56

He heard the Chief say,

"The tree is in the old yard

next to Mrs. Goodkind's house."

"Oh," thought Pickles.

"That's the yard where I lived.

And that's THE TREE."

Pickles jumped up on the truck

with the three firemen.

Away they rode to the yard.

And there, in the wind

and the rain, stood Mrs. Goodkind,

pointing to a very little cat.

The firemen put a ladder

against the tree.

The ladder scared the little cat,

and she ran to a high branch,

where a fireman could not go.

Joe said to Mrs. Goodkind,

"I don't know what to do."

But Pickles knew.

He began to climb the ladder.

Pickles climbed up and up and up.

It was hard work.

But at last he came to the top

of the ladder.

Then he climbed up the tree

until he came to the little cat.

"Come, cat," he said to her.

"Let me help you."

He picked her up
and took her gently
down to Mrs. Goodkind.

Mrs. Goodkind thanked Pickles.

Then she said to him,

"I always knew that someday

you would do big things.

Today you have done

something very big."

Pickles waved a paw at her,

as if to say, "Mrs. Goodkind,

this is only a beginning."

And he rode home to the firehouse—

a proud and happy cat.